ROBOPOP

WRITTEN BY
ALICE HEMMING

ILLUSTRATED BY
JAMES LENT

For Paul

On 'Bring Your Dad to School Day', the dads talked about their jobs. There were:

Bankers and teachers.

Builders and drivers.

Policemen and firemen.

But Dylan and Daisy's dad was different. Nobody understood what he did. And everyone laughed.

"You're not like normal dads,"
said Dylan and Daisy.

"You invent weird gadgets."

"And weirder recipes."

"You know nothing about football."

Dad's smile disappeared.
"Dads don't come in a box," he said.

The next morning, an interesting package appeared.

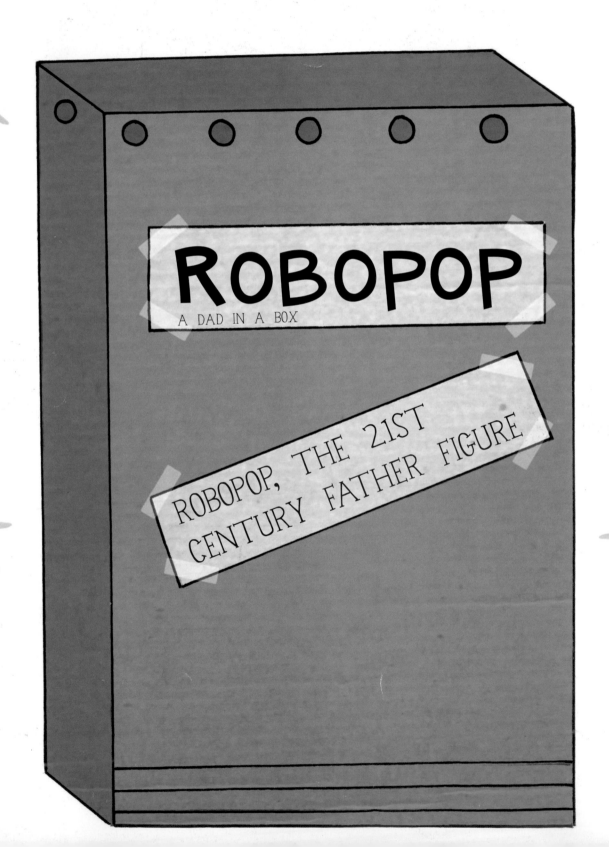

"I'm going out," said Dad. "Meet your babysitter.
All you have to do is switch him on."

Dylan opened the box.

Daisy pressed the ON switch.

Lights flickered, buttons bleeped and the robot opened his eyes.

BLEEP!

"Wow!" said Daisy and Dylan.
"See you later," said Dad.

"I'm RO-BO-POP, your robot pa.
I'm the greatest dad by far.
I play golf and I wear ties.
I catch spiders - any size!"

"Will you take us to football, Robopop?" asked Dylan, "It's a big match today."

"I'm Robopop; I love to play.
We are going to win today."

"It starts in ten minutes!
We'll be late!" said Dylan.

"I'm Robopop and I move fast.
Stick with me; you won't be last."

At the park, Robopop started to warm up.
"Our team never wins," said Daisy.

"Dad says it's more important
to have fun," said Dylan.

So they tried. And Robopop helped.

PASS

At the swings, Robopop helped Daisy jump the queue.

Daisy could see right to the other side of the park.

"Look at all those people!" she said, "There's our neighbour, Mrs Mason. And the other football team. And the little girl from the swings. They look angry!"

"Time to go!" said Dylan.

"Dad's cooking is better than this," whispered Dylan.

"What's for pudding?" asked Daisy.

"Football stars don't eat dessert. Extra spinach will not hurt."

"I'm tired. I want my bath," said Daisy.

"Dad usually reads us a bedtime story," said Dylan.

"Baths and books won't help you score.
Come outside and train some more.
Do five star jumps - make it ten,
then run around the shed again."

"What are we going to do?" said Daisy.

"We managed to switch him on, so surely we can switch him off?" said Dylan.

But Robopop wasn't that easy to catch.

"I'm Robopop and I run fast.
Can't catch me; I'm never last!"

Eventually they got him!

Daisy hit the OFF switch. Lights flickered, buttons bleeped and Robopop closed his eyes.

BLEEP!

Then they spotted someone at the bottom of the garden.

"Dad!" they cried. "We've missed you!"

"You're not like normal dads," said Daisy,
"But you're the best!"
"Yes," said Dylan, "But what will
happen to Robopop?"

"Don't worry," said Dad, "I'm sure we'll think of something..."

The End

Robopop

An original concept by author Alice Hemming

© Alice Hemming

Illustrated by James Lent

Published by MAVERICK ARTS PUBLISHING LTD

Studio 3A, City Business Centre, 6 Brighton Road,

Horsham, West Sussex, RH13 5BB

© Maverick Arts Publishing Limited January 2015 +44 (0)1403 256941

A CIP catalogue record for this book is available at the British Library.

ISBN 978-1-84886-166-4

Maverick
arts publishing
www.maverickbooks.co.uk